MY BODY IS MY TEMPLE

This book is dedicated to Willie Mae and Delores, my grandmothers. They taught me, and all of us, that we are always enough- strong enough, smart enough, pretty enough, capable enough. Even when we pursue more, we are still enough. There is power in never feeling less than...

My name is Nia. My body is God's Temple, but it is also mine. It was given to me, and I take care of it.

Mommy says a Temple is a special place where God lives. I am a special person and God lives in me. In all of us!

I eat healthy foods and I drink my water. I want to be healthy and strong.

These arms are strong for swinging and playing. I swing them, wave them, throw with them and catch with them, most of the time. Okay, maybe I don't catch most of the time, but I sure do try.

I pick up things and I help others.

My community is like my house. I
take care of it.

These legs are strong for walking. I walk
and run. They take me where I need to go,
and I am grateful for my legs.

This face is for smiling. It's precious to those who love me. It is precious to me. I'm strong. I am proud. Nobody values me more than me.

Do you know what else I like about me?

I'm good at things. I am good at sharing. I

am good at learning. I am also good at

listening, again, most of the time.

When I grow up, I am still going to be smart, strong and proud. Why not? I already am!

I think it is nice when other people like

me, but I also like myself. I think it is cool

when someone thinks I am smart or pretty,

but I think so too.

When I get older, I know that boys are going to like me. Why wouldn't they? I'm me. They may even want to kiss me or hug me or, well, movie stuff with me.

They can like me, and I can like them, but my body is my Temple. It is for God and me. When I am all grown up and fall in love and get married, then I can share all of this- all of me. But until then, this is all mine.

I'm not some item at a store to be picked up, used and tossed to the side. If a boy likes me, he'll like talking to me and hanging out with me, not just getting too close to me.

My friend's parents have been married for years and years. Her mom got sick and couldn't really do anything, but her dad still loved her and took care of her. That is the kind of love I want to have one day. I want love that is there even if everything isn't perfect. That love is deeper than touching and kissing and movie stuff.

Boyfriends come and boyfriends go, but my

love for myself is here to stay.

Right now I keep my body healthy, my mind smart, and my room clean, most of the time.

When I get older, I look forward to having friends and people who like me. But if no one likes me, not anybody, not even one person, not even the dog,

I love myself and God loves me.

And that is all that I need.

Made in the USA
San Bernardino, CA
10 October 2017